Disney

BEDTIME STORIES

THE MOVIE STORYBOOK

Adapted by Annmarie Harris
Based on the Screenplay by Matt Lopez and Tim Herlihy
And the Story by Matt Lopez
Executive Producers Adam Shankman, Jennifer Gibgot, Garrett Grant,
Ann Marie Sanderlin
Produced by Adam Sandler, Jack Giarraputo, Andrew Gunn
Directed by Adam Shankman

Copyright © 2008 Disney Enterprises, Inc.

All rights reserved. Published by Disney Press, an imprint of Disney Book Group.

No part of this book may be reproduced or transmitted in any form or by any means, electronic
or mechanical, including photocopying, recording, or by any information storage and retrieval
system, without written permission from the publisher. For information address Disney Press,
114 Fifth Avenue, New York, New York 10011-5690.

Printed in the United States of America

Library of Congress Catalog Card Number on file.

ISBN 978-1-4231-1576-2

Visit www.Disney.com/BedtimeStories

1 3 5 7 9 10 8 6 4 2

DISNEY PRESS
New York

Once upon a time, there was a man named Martin Bronson. "Marty" was the owner and operator of the Sunny Vista motel in Los Angeles. Marty was happy. He loved his work, and he loved his children, Skeeter and Wendy. One of his favorite things to do was to tell them wonderful bedtime stories—and one of their favorite things to do was to listen to them.

Marty ran the motel with the help of Skeeter and Wendy. Skeeter always had ideas for how to make the motel better.

While Marty was a wonderful dad and a splendid host, he was a terrible

businessman. Despite all his work, the Sunny Vista was failing.

One night, after telling an incredible story, Marty put Skeeter to bed and turned out the lights. Just before he fell asleep, Skeeter heard voices coming from his father's office. He crept out of his room to see what was happening. Marty was going to sell the motel to a man named Barry Nottingham! Marty had one condition. He had always dreamed of leaving the motel to his son when he grew up. When Barry promised Marty that he would let Skeeter run the place one day, Marty agreed to the sale.

Thirty years later, Marty's Sunny Vista motel was hard to recognize. It was now the luxurious, high-rise Sunny Vista Nottingham, the finest hotel in Los Angeles. It was where princes and presidents stayed whenever they visited Southern California. And if those princes and presidents needed anything during their stay, they asked for Skeeter Bronson . . . the hotel handyman.

Skeeter had worked his way up to the post of handyman over the years. First he was a parking attendant, then a room-service waiter, then an apprentice handyman, then the assistant handyman, and, finally, the head handyman. He liked his work and the laid-back life that he lived. He got along well with the guests and spent lots of time with his good friend Mickey, a room-service waiter. But he still dreamed of running the hotel one day.

On this particular day, though, Skeeter found himself not at the hotel but rather in his sister Wendy's kitchen. It had been a long time since Skeeter had seen Wendy and her two children; Skeeter and his sister didn't always get along—but when she invited him to her daughter Bobbi's birthday party, he agreed to go.

"Hey, guys!" Skeeter said. "You were pretty young the last time I saw you. Happy birthday, Bobbi."

Patrick, Wendy's son, and Bobbi looked a lot alike: they both had

brown hair like their mother and dark eyes like their dad—but Bobbi was a girl and Patrick was a boy. So when Skeeter handed the present to Patrick, it was clear how little he knew about his niece and nephew.

"*That's* Bobbi," Patrick said, pointing to his sister.

"Whoa, my bad!" Skeeter said.

He gave the gift to Bobbi, who opened it to find a Sunny Vista Nottingham towel and some assorted soaps and shampoos—not exactly a dream gift for a little girl.

Wendy had a special reason for inviting Skeeter to the party. She needed to ask him a favor. The school Bobbi and Patrick attended, which was also where Wendy worked as the principal, was about to shut down. She was being laid off, and she had to go to Arizona for a week to interview for a new job.

"My friend Jill is a teacher at my school, so she can bring the kids in with her in the morning, and then she can watch them until dinnertime," Wendy told her brother. "You'll just have the night shift."

"These guys don't want to hang out with me," Skeeter groaned. Skeeter lived in a cabana at the Sunny Vista Nottingham. There were nights when he was on call for work, and sometimes the kids would need to stay with him at the hotel. Couldn't Wendy's friend Jill watch them the whole time?

"She has night school," Wendy explained.

"Okay, I'll do it." Skeeter sighed. "Good luck on your trip, sis, and I'll see you punks Monday night."

Skeeter headed outside to the green pickup truck he drove. He didn't love the truck—it was huge and old—but it was the only ride he had. When he got to the pickup, a woman with wavy hair was standing there, fuming. She was angry because Skeeter's truck was taking up *two* parking spaces. Skeeter explained that it wasn't his truck—it belonged to the hotel—and he couldn't

get it scratched. That's why he was taking up two spaces.

"You work at a hotel?" the woman asked. "You must be Wendy's brother. I'm her friend Jill—the one who's helping you with the kids next week."

Skeeter was pretty sure teaming up with Jill wasn't going to make babysitting any easier.

An hour later, Skeeter was doing some electrical work at the hotel. The hotel owner, Barry Nottingham, was holding a press conference. Kendall, a snotty hotel manager, hovered over Skeeter, telling him to hurry up. Kendall was one of Skeeter's least favorite people. Before Kendall could say anything else, the hotel owner himself showed up.

"Good to see you again, Mr. Nottingham," Skeeter said, handing over the microphone.

Smiling proudly, Barry announced that he was expanding the Sunny Vista Nottingham. When completed, it would be the largest hotel on the whole West Coast. He explained that in order to expand the hotel, they would have to move to a new site. Those in the room exploded with applause.

"I'm sad to say that our longtime general manager has decided to retire," Barry went on. "So I'm proud to announce the new hotel's manager . . ."

Skeeter straightened up. Was it possible? Was Mr. Nottingham finally fulfilling his promise to Marty and letting Skeeter run the hotel?

". . . Kendall Duncan," Barry finished.

Skeeter couldn't believe Barry's choice for the new manager—and he said so! Little did he know he was standing right next to Barry's daughter, Violet.

The young woman laughed out loud. She'd never heard anyone mock her father that way.

Turning at the sound of Violet's laughter, Skeeter saw that she was beautiful. Just then, Kendall and Mr. Nottingham came over.

"I see you've met my pookie bear," Kendall said as he wrapped his arm protectively around Violet.

"Yes, I have," Skeeter replied, frowning. Then he turned his attention back to Barry. "It's going to be weird to see my father's motel move locations like that, Mr. Nottingham." Even though the Sunny Vista Nottingham was nothing like Marty's old motel, there were still a few remnants of what it was like when Skeeter was a child. Knowing the whole place was going to be torn down made him sad.

"Well, I hope you'll come work for us there," Barry said. "There are going to be a lot of lightbulbs to change."

On Monday, Skeeter arrived at his sister's house for his first night of babysitting. Unable to think of anything to do with the kids, he told them it was bedtime. Ten minutes later, Bobbi and Patrick were sitting on their beds in their pajamas.

"You have to read us a bedtime story," Patrick said as he handed Skeeter some books. Skeeter skimmed through them. They looked terrible—and boring!

"Okay, let me try to make up a story for you, like my old man used to do." He took a deep breath and began. . . .

Skeeter's story was about a magical land and a peasant who lived there. The peasant's name was Sir Fixalot, and despite the fact that he helped people all over the countryside, no one appreciated him.

The land had a king, and the king had a beautiful daughter named Princess Fashionista. The princess had a boyfriend named Sir Buttkiss. No one liked Sir Buttkiss, but he was always nice to the king, so he got everything he wanted.

Skeeter ended the story when Sir Buttkiss inherited the kingdom and Sir Fixalot moved into a shoe and was eaten by crocodiles.

Bobbi and Patrick were mad. That was no way for a story to end!

"It's not fair!" Bobbi protested. "If Sir Fixalot's better than Sir Buttkiss, he should have a chance to prove it."

"Okay, okay," Skeeter said, sitting back down. "Forget everything I said about living in a shoe and crocodiles. What the king *really* said was that there's another worthy man in the kingdom, and it wouldn't be fair unless he got a chance to prove his worth. This man's name was . . . Sir Fixalot!"

"Yay!" Bobbi and Patrick cheered.

"And then it started raining gum balls," Patrick added with a sleepy yawn. "The end."

"Raining gum balls?" Skeeter asked.

"Why not?" Patrick replied. "It's a bedtime story. Anything can happen."

Skeeter couldn't argue with that. He turned out the light and pulled the door closed behind him.

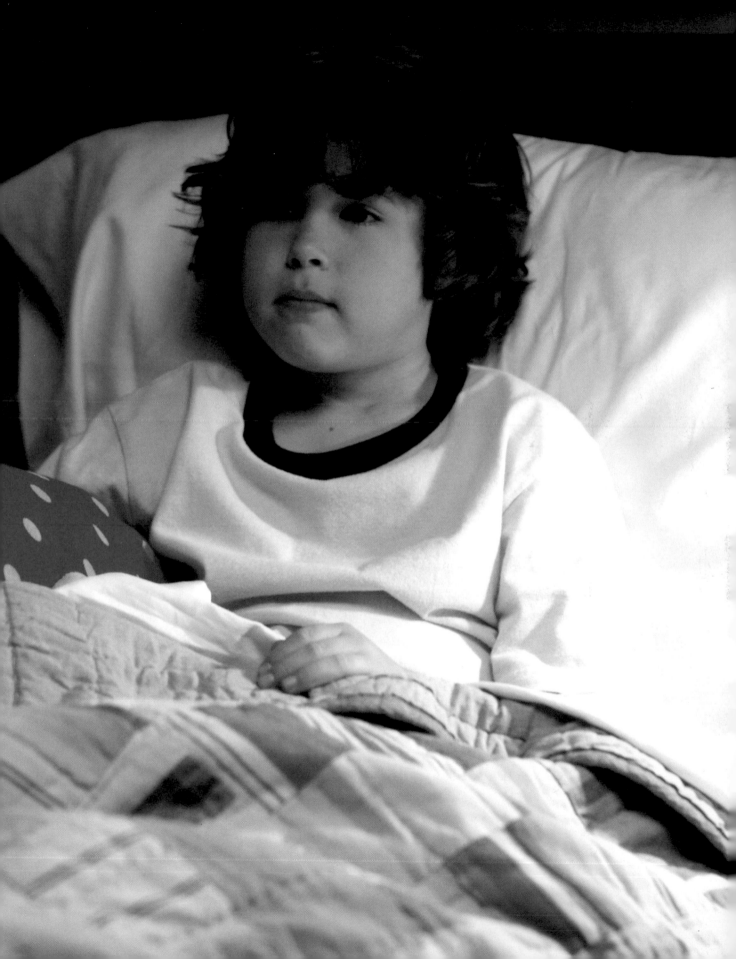

The next day at work, Skeeter was summoned to Mr. Nottingham's suite. While he was there, Mr. Nottingham mentioned the new hotel's secret theme, courtesy of Kendall: rock and roll.

"Oh, you mean like the Hard Rock hotel chain?" Skeeter pointed out.

Mr. Nottingham grew angry. He demanded that Kendall come up with a new idea. Then he told Skeeter that if he could come up with a better theme than Kendall's, he could run the place. The two of them would have to present their ideas to Mr. Nottingham at his birthday party that weekend.

Skeeter couldn't believe his luck. This was his chance!

Later that afternoon, Skeeter was driving home in the pickup truck. Suddenly, something fell through the open sunroof and hit him on the head. It was a blue gum ball! He looked up just in time to see a cascade of rainbow-colored gum balls falling from the sky—just like in his story! Skeeter jumped out of the car and opened an umbrella. The gum balls, meanwhile, continued to rain down from above. He peered out from under the umbrella to see a giant truck tipped over onto its side on an overpass. The side of the truck said, SWEET TOOTH CANDY COMPANY.

Skeeter shook his head. "That's a little spooky."

That night Skeeter was on call, so Bobbi and Patrick came to stay with him at the hotel. After the gum ball experience, Skeeter had an idea for that night's story.

It was about a cowboy named Jeremiah Skeets. Jeremiah rode an old horse, and he felt people didn't take him seriously because of it. So, he headed over to the local used-horse trader, where he made a deal that got him a new horse for free!

"A guy getting a free horse?" Patrick said. "That's not a good story."

"Why can't he do something a real gentleman would do?" Bobbi asked. "Like save a damsel in distress or something." She changed the story. Now Jeremiah had to help Miss Davenport, the daughter of the wealthiest man in the West. She was being attacked by outlaws!

"Right," Skeeter agreed. He added that after Jeremiah saved Miss Davenport, she gave him a hundred-million dollars to thank him.

But Bobbi had a different ending for the story. "Jeremiah can't accept Miss Davenport's money, but she insists on offering him a token of her appreciation—a kiss!"

"Then an angry dwarf kicks him in the butt!" Patrick added. He and Bobbi high-fived and broke into giggles.

Skeeter thought the story was strange, but if it came true like the one from the night before, he'd be satisfied with a new ride and maybe a kiss.

Once the kids were asleep, Skeeter asked his friend Mickey to hang out in the cabana while he drove to the closest sports-car dealership.

It was closed, but there was a man standing in front staring into the showroom window. The man told Skeeter to chew a gum ball, close his eyes, and count to six. When Skeeter opened his eyes, he saw the man running down the street—with his wallet!

"Hey!" Skeeter shouted. "My wallet! That's not how the story ends!"

Sighing, Skeeter climbed into his old pickup truck. As he drove back to the hotel, he came upon a bunch of paparazzi. They had surrounded a woman and were taking her photo incessantly.

Skeeter drove his truck right into the middle of the crowd. When the paparazzi had scattered, Skeeter saw who they were after—Violet Nottingham! He opened the passenger door of his truck and extended his hand, and Violet quickly climbed into the truck.

"My hero!" Violet said. "How can I ever repay you?"

"No thanks necessary, ma'am," Skeeter replied as he escorted Violet to her car.

"Well, I must show my appreciation in some way," Violet said, batting her eyelashes. She leaned in to kiss him. But just as their lips were about to touch, a very short man came running up and kicked Skeeter!

Skeeter went home without a free car, without a kiss, *and* without his wallet! Maybe there was nothing to the stories after all.

The next morning, Skeeter, Bobbi, and Patrick were eating breakfast when Jill came by to pick up the kids. She asked how the night had gone.

"An angry dwarf kicked my butt, and I didn't get a free car," Skeeter said.

"He's talking about our bedtime story," Bobbi explained.

"Uncle Skeeter said Jeremiah would get a new horse and a kiss," Patrick added. "But I said a dwarf would kick his butt."

Suddenly Skeeter had a shocking revelation. The *kids* were controlling the bedtime stories, not him! That's why things hadn't worked out quite the way *he* wanted. He smiled. Tonight would be different.

As the kids were leaving Skeeter's with Jill, Kendall stopped by. "I heard about your hero act with my girlfriend last night," Kendall said. He promised Skeeter that there was no way he would be able to steal Violet *or* the manager position from him.

After his run-in with Skeeter, Kendall decided to go to the site of the new hotel so he could check it out. When he pulled up, he saw that he was in front of a school.

Just then, he noticed Bobbi and Patrick in the school yard. He recognized them as the kids he'd seen leaving Skeeter's place earlier. He had an idea. An evil idea . . .

That night, Bobbi asked for a story with some romance.

Skeeter told one about a great Greek hero named Skeetacus. He was an amazing chariot driver and the founder of the X Games. He and the fairest maiden in the land went on a date.

Then Bobbi and Patrick took over. They explained that Skeetacus and the maiden went to an old tavern where they met all the girls who were mean to Skeetacus when he was growing up. The girls were so jealous of the maiden, they did the Hokey Pokey! Later, Skeetacus and the maiden got caught in the rain and took cover in a cave—and Abe Lincoln was there!

Skeeter wasn't sure if any of Bobbi and Patrick's story would come true, but he hoped the good stuff would.

The next day, Skeeter took a walk by the beach. He called Violet and invited her to lunch, but she was on a private jet to Las Vegas. Skeeter was confused. According to the story, he was supposed to have a date with the fairest maiden in the land. But how could that happen if Violet was out of town?

He was lost in his thoughts when a woman crashed right into him. It was Jill. She was on her lunch break, but she agreed to go with Skeeter to get something to eat. They headed to a place just off the beach. It was empty, except for a group of stylish women sitting at a table.

"Oh, my gosh!" one of them cried. "Is that Skeeter Bronson?"

The women were all people Skeeter had gone to high school with! He convinced Jill to pretend to be his girlfriend, and then he introduced her to everyone.

One of the women looked upset. "We were pretty mean to Skeeter in high school, but now I feel really bad about it." The woman's name was Donna. She took out a business card and gave it to Skeeter. She told him to call her if he ever thought of a way she could make up for treating him so badly in high school.

Suddenly, the other women started doing the Hokey Pokey! Skeeter couldn't believe this was happening!

Back on the beach, Skeeter and Jill began to walk and talk. The conversation turned to Patrick and Bobbi. Skeeter's sister would be home the next day. He only had one more night with the kids! Skeeter hadn't realized they would be going back to their mom so soon. He was going to miss them.

It started raining, so Skeeter and Jill ran for shelter under the boardwalk. It was then that Skeeter realized *Jill* was the fairest maiden in

the land. How could he have missed it? He leaned in to kiss her. As they drew closer, a coin fell through a crack in the boardwalk and landed in front of Skeeter. It was a penny, heads up. *Abe Lincoln's* head up.

"Look," Skeeter said excitedly, holding the penny out to Jill. "We're good now. We can kiss."

But Jill wasn't so sure. "Actually, I think I'd better go," she said, leaving Skeeter alone under the boardwalk.

Later that night, Skeeter began his final bedtime story for Bobbi and Patrick. This tale took place in outer space. . . .

The Supreme Galactic Council was choosing someone to control a new planet. Everyone believed Supreme Leader Baracto favored the evil governor of Hotellium, General Kendallo. But there was a wild card in the mix—Skeeto Bronsonian, the fastest pilot in the Milky Way.

Then Bobbi and Patrick took over. . . .

They explained that Skeeto spoke an alien language that no one understood, and someone always had to translate for him. Then Leader Baracto made Skeeto and Kendallo face off in a no-gravity fight. In the end, Skeeto won the battle! He was made the ruler!

"Kids, you did it," Skeeter told Bobbi and Patrick. "That was the perfect ending for our last story."

"Oh, that's not the end," Patrick said.

"Yeah, that would be too obvious," Bobbi agreed.

"Somebody threw a fireball at Skeeto and he got incinerated," Patrick said.

"The end!" Bobbi added triumphantly. Then she and Patrick collapsed in silly laughter.

"Incinerated?" Skeeter said, horrified. "No!"

The next day, on the way to Mr. Nottingham's party, Kendall stopped for a special meeting with Jill at her school. He thought she should know that her school was going to be torn down by Skeeter's boss. He also lied and said that Skeeter had known about Nottingham's plan all along and hadn't done anything to stop it. Jill was furious! Feeling pleased with himself, Kendall drove to the birthday party.

Skeeter was on his way there, too. But first he stocked up on oven mitts, smoke detectors, sunblock, and flame-resistant Christmas-tree spray. He sprayed his entire body from head to toe before heading to Barry Nottingham's mansion.

The theme of Mr. Nottingham's birthday party was a Hawaiian luau. There were tiki torches and flaming drinks all over the lawn! Skeeter couldn't believe his bad luck! How would he ever be able to avoid incineration here?

Skeeter grabbed a pineapple ice-cream treat from a passing waiter. But when he bit into it, he felt a sharp pain on his tongue. A bee had stung him!

Just then, it was announced that the meeting to discuss ideas for the new hotel would take place inside. Everyone filed into the living room.

"Gentlemen, who would like to go first?" Mr. Nottingham asked.

Skeeter's tongue was so swollen from the bee sting that he couldn't talk, so he just pointed to Kendall. Kendall stepped forward and confidently revealed his idea—a hotel with a musical-theater theme.

"Thank you, Kendall," Mr. Nottingham said when he was finished. "Skeeter, you're up."

"Ibe dug rinkid ow bis . . ." Skeeter began. No one could understand a thing he was saying!

Mickey stepped forward. "He's saying a bee stung his tongue."

"Can you translate his entire presentation?" Barry asked Mickey.

"I can try," Mickey said. He proceeded to translate as Skeeter explained how he had spent the last week seeing the hotel through the eyes of his niece and nephew. Skeeter remembered that, to a kid, everything about staying in a hotel is strange and wonderful, from the bed to the elevator to the lobby. Skeeter's idea was to help guests experience an escape from their everyday lives. He proposed showing guests at the new hotel what every kid knows but every adult forgets: it's fun to try new things.

"That's brilliant," Barry said warmly. "Congratulations! You've just won the keys to the kingdom, my boy."

Kendall walked over to Skeeter.

"Congratulations," Kendall said. "You deserve it, pal. You've got an iron will. I wouldn't have the guts to knock down the school where my niece and nephew went, where my sister was principal, and where my girlfriend taught!"

"What are you talking about?" Skeeter asked, confused. His tongue was better, but now his head didn't feel right.

"That's where the hotel is going," Kendall said smugly, and then he walked away.

Skeeter was still trying to process what he had just learned when Mr. Nottingham came over to congratulate him.

"Good show, son," the hotel owner told him. "The bee-sting language really worked for you on a sympathetic level."

"Sir, I really need to speak with you for a second—" Skeeter began, but he was drowned out by the sound of the crowd singing "Happy Birthday." Waitresses dressed as hula girls entered the room carrying a huge cake with hundreds of burning candles on it. At the same time, Hawaiian dancers spun torches of fire. Skeeter became more and more panicked. Finally, he couldn't take it anymore. He pulled out a fire extinguisher and sprayed it at the cake and, unfortunately, at Mr. Nottingham.

"Bronson, you're fired!" Mr. Nottingham bellowed.

Skeeter shook his head in disbelief. "Fired," he said. "Now I get it."

Skeeter wasn't upset. True, he'd lost his job, but he now knew there were more important things—like his sister and her kids . . . and Jill. He needed to do something to help them.

He hopped in the truck and drove to Wendy's school. Jill was there, but she was so angry she refused to see him. Skeeter saw Bobbi and Patrick in the hallway. They couldn't believe what Jill had told them about their uncle.

"We thought you were always supposed to be the good guy," Bobbi said.

"Yeah, me, too," Skeeter said as the kids walked away. Skeeter had to

figure out how to be the hero. But what was he going to do?

The next day, Jill met Mr. Nottingham on the steps of the town's city hall. She begged him to reconsider his plan to tear down the school. Couldn't he find another site for his hotel?

Jill followed Mr. Nottingham into the zoning commissioner's office, hoping she could change his mind. They were both surprised to find Skeeter there, sitting opposite Donna Hynde, the zoning commissioner—and the woman who had given Skeeter her card earlier that week! It was *her* job to give Mr. Nottingham the permit he needed to tear down the school.

43

"Mr. Bronson came here to bring up several interesting points before I made any hasty decisions," Donna explained to Mr. Nottingham. "I'm afraid your application for a variance has been denied."

"But don't worry," Skeeter added, "Donna and I found a great property for auction on the beach in Santa Monica."

"Beachside property?" Mr. Nottingham asked. "I'm okay with that." He immediately tried to call off the demolition of the school, but when he called, he couldn't reach Kendall.

Skeeter and Jill dashed out of city hall. They needed to find a way to get to the school—fast! But Skeeter didn't have the truck anymore—the hotel had taken it back—and Jill had been in such a hurry when she arrived, she parked in a tow-away zone. Her car was being taken away! But then Skeeter saw two bikers getting hot dogs from a street vendor.

"Come on!" Skeeter called out to Jill. They jumped on one of the motorcycles and sped off toward the school.

Down at the school, a number of parents, teachers, and students had gathered to protest the demolition. Wendy was back, and she'd come to the protest with Bobbi and Patrick. The kids had made a banner that read: THIS SKOOL IS AWESOME! They were planning to hang it up.

Kendall was ready to give the demolition workers the okay. He had turned off his cell phone to avoid any interference with the radio-controlled explosives.

Suddenly, Wendy realized that Bobbi and Patrick were no longer at her side. They had disappeared!

Patrick and Bobbi hadn't really vanished—they had gone inside the school to find the perfect place to hang their banner. "When the demolition guys see this banner hanging in the window, they'll change their minds," Bobbi said. Outside, Kendall began the countdown, unaware of the danger to the two children.

"Wait!" Wendy cried, frantic. But Kendall refused to wait.

Just then, Skeeter pulled up on the motorcycle and stopped Kendall from demolishing the school. The crowd cheered wildly as Bobbi and Patrick came running out of the building.

"They decided not to blow up the school," Wendy said, hugging her children.

"But we didn't even get to hang our sign," Patrick said, disappointed.

"They heard about it, and that was enough to make them stop," Skeeter said. "You guys are heroes."

Skeeter and his friends and family did well after that. Wendy remained the principal of the school, and Bobbi and Patrick continued to go there. Jill stayed at the school as a teacher, and Skeeter opened up his own hotel with a little help from Mr. Nottingham. He called it Marty's Motel, after his dad.

And Skeeter and Jill? Well, of course, they lived happily ever after.